How Much Farther, Papa Smurf?

For Demi Rizzo, the smurfiest kid in the village
—R.P.

To my brothers CJ, Rob, and Nick. Your support makes me feel like I can achieve
anything. Know that each of you is endlessly great in your own way
—M.D.

Library of Congress Control Number: 2021952889
ISBN 978-0-06-307797-3

The artist used Adobe Photoshop to create the digital illustrations for this book.
Typography by Elaine Lopez-Levine
22 23 24 25 26 PC 10 9 8 7 6 5 4 3 2 1
❖
First Edition

THE SMURFS

How Much Farther, Papa Smurf?

Written by
ROBB PEARLMAN

Illustrated by
MELANIE DEMMER

HARPER
An Imprint of HarperCollins Publishers

I hate clouds.

One morning, Papa Smurf stood in the center of the Smurf Village.
"Gather round, Smurfs!" he said. "Tonight, we'll get to see
something that hardly ever happens: a Blue Moon!"

"But Papa," said Brainy Smurf, "we'll *never* see the moon
with so many clouds in the sky!"

"I hate clouds," muttered Grouchy, folding his arms.

"You're right, Brainy," said Papa Smurf. "But we *will* be able to see the Blue Moon if we make our way *above* the clouds!"

"How do we do that?" asked Smurfette.

Papa Smurf held up a map. "All we have to do is smurf our way to the top of the mountain! And once we get there, we can have a campout! This straight path will take us from where we are to where we want to be. But let's leave soon. You never know what we'll smurf along the way!"

Everyone went home and packed
their sleeping bags and what they
thought they would need for the trip.

When the Smurfs reached the edge of their village, Brainy used his fingers to measure the distance of the trip on the map.

"How much farther, Papa Smurf?" he asked.

"Not far now, Brainy," said Papa Smurf, "if we follow the straight path."

But before they could go any farther, Smurfette skipped off the path and climbed up a tall tree.

"I can see the Village from up here!" The other Smurfs hurried up the tree. It really was a spectacular view! Grouchy stayed put on the ground.

I hate high places!

Soon the Smurfs were on their way again. They walked deep into the forest and found a patch of smurfberries.

"How much farther, Papa Smurf?" asked Brainy.

"Not far now!" he replied, "if we follow the straight path."

"Let's pick smurfberries!" said Farmer.

"We'll help," said Handy, who had brought along his smurfberry pickers.

"The shortest distance between two points is a straight line," said Brainy. "If we keep veering off the path we'll never get there!"

"I hate never getting anywhere," grumbled Grouchy.

Once they had picked lots of smurfberries, Papa Smurf said, "Okay, Smurfs, let's get smurfing!"

The Smurfs kept walking and reached a beautiful grassy meadow.

"How much farther, Papa Smurf?" asked Brainy.

"Not far now!" Papa replied, "if we follow the straight path."

"This looks like the perfect picnic spot!" said Chef. "Why don't I smurf up some lunch?"

While Chef laid out the picnic,
the other Smurfs played

smurf the flag,

hide-and-go-smurf,

and Simon smurfs.

But not Brainy. He didn't want to play or have lunch. All he wanted to do was follow the straight path and get to the mountaintop.

Once the games were played and every belly was full, Papa Smurf said, "Okay, Smurfs, let's get smurfing!"

The Smurfs found a stream and a field of wildflowers.
"How much farther, Papa Smurf?" asked Brainy.
"Not far now!" he replied.

"Let's go for a swim!" said Hefty, who was always happy to exercise.
Brainy tried to tell everyone that they would get to the mountaintop
quicker if they just stayed on the straight path, but they were all
laughing and having too much fun to hear him.

While they splashed, snorkeled, and soaked, Vanity searched for just the right wildflower for his hat.

Once everyone was dried off, Papa Smurf said, "Okay, Smurfs, let's get smurfing!"

And Brainy kept asking,

"How much farther,
Papa Smurf?"

"How much farther,
Papa Smurf?"

And each time, Papa would say,
"Not far now!"

Until finally, Brainy demanded, "Is it much farther, Papa Smurf?"
"Yes, it is!" Papa exclaimed.

"Sometimes the smurfiest part of a journey is not the straight path that takes you to where you want to be, it's what you get to smurf along the way!" said Papa Smurf. "And if you're having fun, that can take time."

Handy used his ruler to measure the distance between where they were and the mountaintop.

"Brainy's right," said Handy. "If we follow the straight path without smurfing around, we'll get there quickly!"

"If that's really what you want to do . . ." said Papa Smurf.

I hate taking time.

Let's get there already!

So the Smurfs followed the straight path.
Past the carousel.

Past the Forest Games.

And past the concert.

They didn't stop until they reached the mountaintop.

And Brainy was right—they did get there very quickly.

The clouds floated in the sky below.

The stars and the biggest, most beautiful,
bluest moon they'd ever seen rose in the sky above.

As the Smurfs snuggled into their sleeping bags, Papa could hear them talk about all the fun they had on their way to see the big, beautiful Blue Moon.

"Those were the sweetest smurfberries I'd ever eaten!"

"That was the smurfiest game ever!"

"Brainy's way *was* quicker," said Grouchy, "but it was *a lot* less fun than Papa's."

"The only thing better than being here," said Smurfette, "was getting here!"

"I'm glad you had fun today, my Smurfs. Let's come back here for the next Blue Moon!"

Brainy tried to stay awake. He had one more question to ask.
"How much longer until the *next* Blue Moon, Papa Smurf?"
"Not very long, Brainy."

"Not very long at all."